## Kids love reading
## *Choose Your Own Adventure*®!

"These books are like games.
Sometimes the choice seems like it
will solve everything, but you wonder
if it's a trap."
Matt Harmon, age 11

"I think you'd call this a book for active
readers, and I am definitely an
active reader!"
Ava Kendrick, age 11

"You decide your own fate,
but your fate is still a surprise."
Chun Tao Lin, age 10

"Come on in this book if you're crazy
enough! One wrong move and
you're a goner!"
Ben Curley, age 9

"You can read Choose Your Own
Adventure books so many wonderful
ways. You could go find your dog
or follow a unicorn."
Celia Lawton, 11

## Ask your bookseller for books you have missed or visit us at cyoa.com to collect them all.

# ZOMBIE PENPAL

BY KEN MCMURTRY

ILLUSTRATED BY WES LOUIE
COVER ILLUSTRATED BY KEITH NEWTON

CHOOSECO®
WAITSFIELD, VERMONT

Illustrated by: Wes Louie
Cover Art: Keith Newton
Cover Design: Dot Greene
Book design: Stacey Boyd, Big Eyedea Visual Design

For information regarding permission, write to:

**CHOOSECO**
P.O. Box 46
Waitsfield, Vermont 05673
www.cyoa.com

ISBN-13: 978-1-933390-34-5
ISBN-10: 1-933390-34-4

Published simultaneously in the United States and Canada

Printed in the United States

0 9 8 7 6 5 4 3 2 1

*This book is dedicated to*
*Kaitlyn Ann Shannon*
*who at age one perfected the zombie walk.*

# BEWARE and WARNING!

This book is different from other books.

You and YOU ALONE are in charge of what happens in this story.

The wrong decision could end in peril—even death. But don't despair. At any time, YOU can go back and make another choice, alter the path of your story, and change its result. Zombies, their controlling bokors, the charms and protective spells of Voodoo and the occult all mix in every day life in New Orleans. You learn all about it from your penpal Sam. But then Katrina comes and Sam stops writing. Did she disappear during the terrible floods following the hurricane? You are sure you will never know until a new girl shows up at your school in Pointy Hill, Maine who reminds you of your penpal. Her name is Rose but is she really Sam? You'll have to tread carefully to find out. Because if Rose is really a zombie, there is danger for everyone involved...

April 2005

Dear Penpal,

How are you? I am fine. My baptism name is Samosa Rose Desjardine. But my friends call me Sam. I live with my grandma. I call her Mammaw. We live in New Orleans. Louisiana. I am in the second grade at Evergreen School. Our class project is to learn about different states. I picked Maine. I got your name and address from the penpal club. I want to learn about you and about your state of Maine. Is there a hill in Pointy Hill where you are?

Please write back and tell me if you will be my penpal.

Your new friend,

Sam Desjardine

May 2005

Dear Penpal,

Thank you for writing me. I liked learning about the giant crawdads you call lobsters. Also your famous Bean store. The picture of the lobster was kind of scary. Are they red like that when you catch them? How do you eat them?

You asked about me. I live with Mammaw in a small blue house. It is near the French quarter in our city. We like to take walks down by the Mississippi on River Walk. Music is very popular here and famous. Sometimes we get big rain storms but not snow. I am sending along some alligator jerky for you to try. Write soon!

Your friend,

Sam

P.S. What do they sell at the Bean store besides beans?

July 2005

Dear Penpal,

You asked about New Orleans. It is fun living here. There is a streetcar near our house. Mammaw drinks coffee and eats fried dough for breakfast. The fried dough is called a beignet. You say Ben-Yay. Every year there is a big parade called Mardi Gras here. People go a little crazy. The music is nice and loud.

Mammaw won't let me go into some stores here. They sell things like black candles and herbs and potions. She calls them Voodoo shops and says I must not visit them. One of the stores is called the Seven Wonders Shop of Voodoo. It is owned by our neighbor Wonder Samedi. Wonder seems like a nice man but he has a friend called Mary who never smiles. She is a teacher at Evergreen.

Hope your summer is fun. It is hot and steamy here.

Write soon, your friend,

Sam

P.S. I am sending a picture of myself so you will know what I look like. Please send me a picture of you.

August 28, 2005

Dear Penpal,

There is a big storm coming. I am very scared. The storm is named Katrina. It is a hurricane level 5. It is raining hard already. The wind is blowing at sixty-miles per hour. And the worst part of Katrina is coming tomorrow...

The mayor went on TV and said that New Orleans will be flooded. We are all supposed to leave the city and go to higher ground. But Mammaw says no. She says that she is not about to give up everything and walk away.

Instead we are going over to see Wonder Samedi's house. Remember him? He has that strange shop. They say Wonder Samedi is a bokor. Bokor is the word for voodoo priest. Mammaw says he can cast a spell to protect us. I think we should just leave. I am so frightened.

I have to go. Mary the woman who never smiles, is here to take us to the voodoo ceremony. Pray for us please.

Signed by your friend,

Sam

*Several years later...*

You are hanging out with your two best friends, Elton and Mina, at your house in Pointy Hill, Maine. It is autumn term break at Dragonfly School where you are all in 7th grade. The three of you get together every Friday night to watch horror films. But because of vacation you've moved up Monster Movie Night to Monster Movie Afternoon. On TV, a woman in a vampire costume is introducing the film called *Return of the Bride of Frankenstein*.

"Is something bugging you?" Mina suddenly blurts out, scooping another handful of buttered popcorn from the bowl between you on the couch. "You seem quiet."

"Well, sort of," you reply. "You know that new girl, the one named Rose?"

*Turn to page 2.*

**2**

"You mean the one who looks and acts like a zombie?" Elton asks.

"What do you mean, Elton?" Mina laughs. "Rose is not a zombie."

"Wanna bet?" Elton answers. "Her eyes are dark pools of black. She walks around in a trance most of the time. And her skin is really pale. I tell you she's a zombie."

Elton might have a point, but that is not what is bothering you.

"Rose reminds me of someone. I just don't know who."

"Somebody you know?" Mina asks.

"Or some zombie you know?" Elton suggests. Mina jabs Elton with her elbow.

"Sam!" you say suddenly. The name is out of your mouth before the thought has even formed in your head. "That's it. She reminds me of Sam. Sam Desjardine. My old penpal from New Orleans in second grade."

*Go on to the next page.*

"The one who died in Katrina?" Elton says help-fully.

"I don't know that she died," you reply. "I just never heard from her again. I tried writing a bunch of times but every letter came back marked 'Addressee Unknown.'"

The wind outside suddenly gusts, and some leaves snap at the window.

Elton points outside, "Speak of the devil. If you want to ask Rose the zombie if she's really Sam Desjardine, now's your chance. There she goes."

*Turn to page 4.*

**4**

You and Mina stand to look. The new girl named Rose passes by Elton's house on a bike. You watch as she rides straight into the cemetery next door.

"What is she going to do in the cemetery in this weather?" Mina asks.

"I don't know but I'm going to follow her and find out," you reply.

You head out the front door and your friends follow. "I'm not sure this is a good idea," Elton says.

"Shut up, Elton," Mina shouts over the wind.

You pass through the old iron gates to the cemetery. It's getting dark and the storm they have been predicting is about to hit. Dark clouds roll across the sky. Drops of rain begin to splatter. When you come to a fork in the main path, it's hard to see any bike tracks. Then you hear a scraping sound off to the right.

*If you follow the scraping sound, turn to page 7.*

*If you stay on the main path and go straight ahead, turn to page 35.*

"The noise is coming from deep in the grave-yard," you say, "up near the top of the cemetery."

"Who would be up there with dark coming and a storm raging?" Mina shouts over the wind.

"Let's not find out," Elton says.

"Are you afraid?" Mina asks.

"Yes," Elton says. "I want to get out of here," he adds.

"But we can't go back now!" Mina says.

"I can," Elton says. "I live next door. Besides I think I suffer from cemeteryphobia."

"Oh, stop whining. So you're afraid of ceme-teries—so what? You'll miss the fun," Mina snorts. She turns around in your direction nodding, "I'm with you."

You forge ahead with Mina right behind. You notice out of the corner of your eye Elton sticks with you after all. Mina probably embarrassed him into it, you think.

*Turn to page 8.*

# 8

Pointy Hill's cemetery is old. A few stone mausoleums stand out like overweight garden sheds in the moonlight. The whole cemetery is surrounded by a fancy wrought iron fence, topped with twisting vines and cherub faces. It has stopped raining, the wind is a whisper now. The crops of gravestones are slick with moisture.

You hear it again. A scuffing, scraping sound followed by a soft "plomp."

"What is it?" Elton asks.

"Beats me. We'll have to get closer," you reply. Elton looks like he doesn't like that idea much.

Using maples, willows and a crumbling tombstone to hide, you edge toward the sound. An owl sits atop a tomb, waiting for night mice to appear. The silhouette of the magnificent bird reminds you that the world of night is different. It's secret. You need always be on guard.

"Look," Mina whispers.

The nearly full moon emerges from behind a cloud. The sudden light reveals a man standing up ahead holding a shovel. His jacket is draped over a headstone while he wipes sweat from his forehead. A large mound of dirt is piled on a tarp beside the open grave.

"Isn't that Professor Samuels?" you ask.

"It looks like him," Elton says.

*Turn to page 10.*

"It can't hurt to check out that noise. And Sam couldn't have gone far," you say.

You move toward the sound, threading your way past the old moss-covered tombs and mausoleums.

*Turn to page 8.*

# 10

His name might be Ralph Samuels, but all the kids at school call him "Professor Gaga." Some kids even call him that to his face. Professor Gaga is a little out of touch most of the time. You suspect he likes the nickname. In class he's always talking about his laboratory. It's in the attic of his house. He pronounces it La-Bore-a-Tory. His nose is always buried in some book about science or alchemy or the X-Files.

"It is him," Mina says.

"In science class last week," you say to Elton, "you asked about zombies. And about Frankenstein, and the science behind the reanimation stuff. How far fetched is all that?"

"Remember how Professor Gaga overheard and said it wasn't such a nutty idea?" Mina chimes in.

"That's because of everything we know now about genetics and cell regeneration biology," Elton adds. "He's correct."

Elton reminds you a little of Gaga sometimes. But you keep that thought to yourself for now.

"You don't think he's...." before you can finish your sentence, the professor drops out of sight. He has jumped into the grave! A moment later a crowbar flies out of the hole. The professor, grunting with the load, pushes a very large rolled up rug onto the grass. Climbing out himself, the professor brushes the dirt from his clothes. He pulls up a small wooden ladder from the grave and begins to fill the hole.

*Turn to page 12.*

"Oh. My. God. He's stealing a body," Mina says.

"That's sure what it looks like," you say.

"I always thought he was a sicko," Elton adds.

After the hole is filled and the sod replaced, the professor drags the heavy rug to the back of his Volvo station wagon. With some difficulty, he manages to get the bundle into the back. Quickly, he loads the rest of his equipment, the shovel, the ladder, and the tarp. He grabs his jacket and gets in the car. He clearly wants to avoid detection. Next he lets the brake off so he can coast silently down the hill and out the cemetery exit.

You creep from your hiding spot and approach the newly filled grave. Just as you thought, "Look, Mina," you say. "This is Mr. Angel's grave."

"Our former wood shop teacher?" Elton cries, horrified.

"What on earth is Gaga going to do with a dead wood shop teacher?" Mina asks.

"I have no idea," you reply. "But we need to do something."

---

*You know where Professor Gaga lives. If you decide to go to his house, and find out what he is up to, go on to the next page.*

*If you decide to look for Gaga at Dragonfly school, where he has been known to work on late night experiments, turn to page 56.*

*This is too weird. If you decide it's time to call in the Marines and seek outside help, turn to page 43.*

Professor Gaga lives in an old Victorian style house. The paint is peeling, and two of the upstairs windows are broken and covered with cardboard. The small front porch creaks when you step on it. The front door hangs crooked on its hinges. You notice fresh tire tracks leading to his closed garage.

"I think we need the element of surprise. So I am not going to knock, if that's okay with you two," you say to your friends. Elton and Mina glance at each other, and nod okay. You nod back and turn the front door knob. The door swings open with a loud creak.

You tiptoe inside. Mina and Elton follow. A crack of light comes from beneath a door in one of the back rooms. Moving as quietly as possible you make your way past a living room scattered with books and papers. In the kitchen, moldy dishes, cups with blue fungus growing in them and greasy plates are scattered around the counters. A black cat sits on the kitchen table lapping a bowl of cream. When you pass the cat it arches its back.

"Black cat," Mina whispers. "Nice touch Gaga."

"Very funny," Elton hisses.

*Turn to page 14.*

# 14

You open the door with the light underneath noiselessly. It leads upstairs to an attic lab. A smell, like rotten meat, is strong. You hold your nose as the three of you begin to ascend the stairs.

"It sounds like Professor Gaga is talking to someone," Mina whispers.

You pause to listen.

"You'll be right as rain in no time," you hear Gaga say. "Although Mr. Angel, I don't think they'll let you operate a band saw ever again. Not after your little accident in woodshop last week."

"Rain?" someone drones in response.

"If I said it almost killed you I would be wrong," Professor Gaga says, "It *did* kill you Mr. Angel."

"Rain?" the weird voice repeats.

"It's just an expression," Gaga replies. "I don't know what's so right about rain, really. I've always found rain a bit of a bother, like tonight when I got soaked digging you up."

"The woodshop is dry," the drone voice says.

You whisper, "If that's Mr. Angel, he sounds like he's auditioning for a Frankenstein movie."

*Go on to the next page.*

"Do you hear what you're saying?" Mina asks. "That can't be Mr. Angel. Mr. Angel is dead."

"But I recognize his voice," you reply. "Mr. Angel has always sounded like Frankenstein, even when he was alive."

A noise at the top of the stairs causes all three of you to jerk.

"My, my, my. Visitors. What are you three doing here?" Professor Gaga asks. He stands at the top of the stairs looking down at you. "I thought I heard some rats scurrying around. Now that you are here, don't be shy, come on up. You're just in time to witness a scientific breakthrough that will astound you. I promise."

*If you decide to accept this bizarre invitation to be astounded (or worse) turn to page 17.*

*You decide to get out of there and return to the cemetery to look for Rose the new girl, turn to page 38.*

You, Mina and Elton climb Gaga's creaky attic stairs.

"I know the ventilation leaves something to be desired," Gaga says, "but science is like beauty. It requires sacrifice."

You don't like the way Gaga says that, but you keep your mouth shut and look around the dim room. There are three stainless steel tables in a row. Your recently deceased shop teacher, Mr. Angel, sits on one of them. The metal table looks shiny and cold. Come to think of it, Mr. Angel looks a little shiny and cold too. A gutter runs around the outer edge of the table with a hose attached leading to a floor drain.

The two other tables hold lab apparatus, test tubes, microscopes, Bunsen burners, some with bubbling beakers atop stands, and spectrometers. In one corner of the lab are two large empty wire crates large enough to hold a big animal. Or even a human.

"What's with the live globes?" Elton asks Gaga, his curiosity overcoming his fear. He points to three round glass orbs—two green ones, and one white—with what appear to be miniature thunder storms raging inside. They sit next to a curled piece of copper wiring. The hiss of small electrical zaps fills the background.

*Turn to page 18.*

# 18

"More like what's with Mr. Angel?" you say, pointing.

Your old shop teacher has gotten off the table and started wandering around the lab. His walk is stiff and mechanical. He is wearing tan carpenter's pants with several pockets. A leather utility belt around his waist holds a nail gun, nails, and a small power drill.

*They buried him with his tools?*

Angel moves like a wind-up toy, bouncing off of things, each bounce sending him off in a new direction.

"The laboratory smell is a small cost to pay for my marvelous discovery," Professor Gaga says, ignoring Elton's question about the hissing orbs. "It is the smell of many experiments. You might even say the smell of success. Look here," he says holding up a gerbil with two missing legs. "Only two days ago this small creature was involved in a fatal accident with my lab fan."

"You mean 'near fatal accident' don't you?" you inquire politely. "That gerbil is alive."

"He's alive, quite right," the professor says. "But he was dead the day before yesterday. Loosing two legs cost him his life. He bled out after his unfortunate encounter with the fan. Now, Lazarus, that's his name, can only run in looping left circles."

*Go on to the next page.*

"You brought Lazarus the gerbil back to life?" Elton asks.

"Thanks to my discovery," Professor Gaga says, "he is indeed alive again."

"How can that be?" you ask taking a closer look at the two-legged gerbil.

"Well there are many factors," Professor G. answers. "First, Lazarus was found while still fresh, right after his accident. I probably should have stitched his legs back on but I was so excited about finding a fresh specimen that I overlooked the obvious."

"You've tried to revive other creatures?" Mina asks.

"Several," Gaga replies, his eyes sparkling. "The longer they have been dead, the briefer the reanimation. I once restored a dead mouse, named Jerry, who had been dead two weeks. He lasted close to four minutes after resurrection. Mr. Peepers, my cat, had chewed Jerry pretty badly. The point is, after a brief period of shaking off *rigor mortis*, Jerry sat up and ate muenster cheese for three minutes. Thanks, that is, to this," Gaga holds up a small vial of purple liquid. "My reanimation serum!"

*Turn to page 20.*

"So, you're not really sure how long the serum will keep something alive?" you ask.

"No, but Lazarus has been going strong for two days now. I've made some adjustments to the formula. I think this discovery just might win me the Nobel Prize. Imagine."

"So the smells in here are your mistakes?" Elton sniffs.

"That's one way of explaining them," Gaga says.

*I don't want to know the other ways of explaining them.*

Professor Gaga points out several glass lab bottles filled with liquid. Small creatures float inside the specimen jars—a bug-eyed rabbit missing both ears, a bird without a head, a bright red lobster, and a variety of damaged insects and snakes. "These are a few of my failures," he says.

"Looks like you've found a way to create zombie pets," you offer.

"Please," the professor begins, "you're over-looking the big picture: reanimation after death. The market will be huge!"

"Not if it makes you a zombie," Elton points out. "Don't your subjects crave fresh brains?"

Before the professor can answer you hear the downstairs door slam shut.

*Go on to the next page.*

Everyone looks around. *Uh-oh.*

"Where is Mr. Angel?" you ask.

"He's gone," Mina says.

"Wow, this is just great," Elton says. "Our zombie shop teacher is loose on the town."

"Angel's gone!?" Professor Gaga cries. "We must find him. ASAP! News of my accomplishments must be kept quiet."

News of Gaga's accomplishments are the *least* of his worries, you think.

*If you decide to go look for Mr. Angel,*
*turn to page 22.*

*If you convince Gaga he has to call in help,*
*turn to page 29.*

You make a quick decision.

"There's no time to call for help," you announce. "We need to go after Mr. Angel before he hurts himself."

"Can zombies hurt themselves? I mean, I thought that it was kind of the point? That a zombie doesn't feel pain?" Elton asks.

"Quit stalling for time, Elton!" Mina says, one step behind as you run from the attic. "Besides, Mr. Angel might hurt someone else!"

You dash out onto Professor Gaga's creaky front porch. There's no sign of Mr. Angel on the front lawn. From the way Gaga gasps and puffs his way after you, it's pretty obvious that his la-bore-a-tory has kept him out of the gym.

"Whatever you do," Gaga wheezes, "don't tell anyone my secret! I beg of you!"

"Was the garage door open when we got here?" Elton asks.

"No!" Mina answers. "But it is now."

You hear a car peeling out at the end of Gaga's street.

"Zombies can drive?" Elton asks.

*Go on to the next page.*

"Come on!" you yell, setting off after the car at a sprint.

You run up the street. The storm is over, but it's now pitch black out. At the end of the lane, you look in both directions for Gaga's beat-up Volvo.

"Is that him?" Mina points. A car is turning the corner. Otherwise the street looks empty.

"Do you think he went back to the cemetery?" Elton asks. "Where would you go if you came back from the dead?"

"Maybe he returned home?" Mina suggests. "But that's in the opposite direction. I think."

"If he went home, Mrs. Angel is about to get the shock of her life," you add.

"Wow, this is great," Elton says rubbing his hands together happily. "A real zombie hunt."

*If you decide to head back to the cemetery to look for Mr. Angel, turn to page 24.*

*If you look up Mr. Angel's address and go there, turn to page 111.*

# 24

You decide to head back to the cemetery. If Mr. Angel isn't there, you can try his house. But sure enough, the dented blue Volvo wagon is crashed in the ditch just outside the Pointy Hill cemetery entrance.

"He's here!" Mina exclaims.

The three of you hurry inside—it's now officially closed—and run toward where you heard the scraping sound. Turning the corner you see a familiar tall figure standing on a stone path. He's illuminated by the round silver light of the moon. A crow perches on a branch nearby. Along the path, small yellow rosettes bloom in the grass, fall dandelions.

"Mr. Angel?" you say, "We came to help you."

"In the cemetery," Mr. Angel says, his voice sounds flat, tired, a dead monotone, "the milkweed pods are starting to open."

"What can we do?" Elton says to you and Mina.

"I want to go home," the zombie shop teacher says.

"We'll help you," Mina offers. "Where's home?" Then she whispers, "Look at his leg."

The left thigh has been torn from Mr. Angel's pants. In fact the thigh itself is gone, only some ragged cloth and a piece of bone remains.

*Turn to page 26.*

"The red maples have peaked," Mr. Angel continues in his monotone. "I love early autumn when the red maples peak."

"Do you want to go to your house?" Elton asks.

"No. I want to go where I belong. I want to sleep again," Mr. Angel says, "The Big Sleep."

"You got that one right buddy," Elton replies.

Mr. Angel is carrying a shovel from Gaga's car. He gets to his tombstone and begins to dig. Mina returns to the old Volvo and brings back three more shovels so all of you can help. As soon as his coffin is exposed, Mr. Angel hops in and lays down inside of it.

"Tell Gaga I'm sorry. I was a bad zombie," Mr. Angel says. He places a handkerchief over his face and closes the coffin.

"Is that our signal to start filling the hole?" Elton whispers.

"I'm not sure I can do this," Mina says. "It feels like I'm burying someone alive."

"Let's put on enough dirt so he can't escape, and go get the cops," you suggest.

*Go on to the next page.*

Your friends agree. You quickly fill the grave with a couple feet of dirt. Then you run back to the cemetery entrance. For some reason, all three of you start laughing. And you can't stop. Even when you see the flashing light of a cop car right next to Gaga's Volvo wagon.

"Can you three tell me what's so funny about stealing a car?" the cop asks.

"Stealing a car? We didn't steal this car!" you cry.

"That's not what Professor Samuels said," the cop answers. "He called it in a half hour ago. Why don't you all come with me to the station and explain what happened? You can start at the beginning."

**The End**

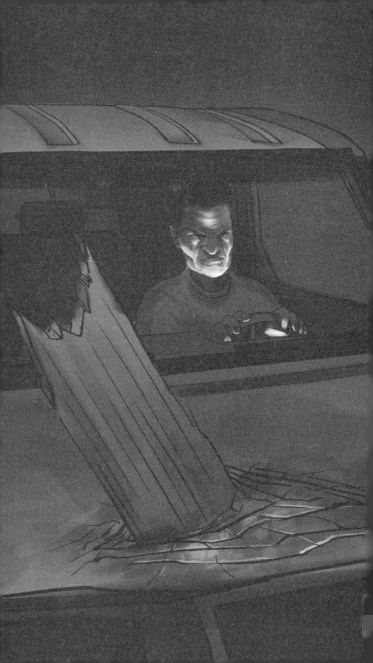

"There's a zombie running loose in the neighborhood," you plead. "We need to call the police."

"Make that a zombie on the loose with a nail gun," Elton adds.

"The police? In Pointy Hill? Get real. More like the National Guard," Mina says, "Where is the phone?"

Professor Gaga looks stunned. "I'm not ready to publish my findings," he says. "We can't get outsiders involved. It's too early. They will steal my ideas."

"You're not making sense, Professor," you say. "Mr. Angel could be dangerous."

"Only to himself," Gaga replies. Then with disdain, "He's always been such a klutz."

You hear the sound of a car starting, then the sound of wood splintering. You get to the window just in time to see Mr. Angel driving away in a red Honda Element.

"He's taking the Element!" Gaga yells, suddenly springing to life and running down the stairs. "I need that for special ceremonies!"

"He can afford two cars on a teacher's salary?" Elton asks as the three of you follow the crazy scientist.

*Turn to page 30.*

"Quick! Do you have a GPS unit in the car?" you ask Professor Gaga

"GPS?" Gaga replies, puzzled.

"Great," Mina says, shaking her head. "He can bring the dead back to life but he doesn't know what GPS stands for."

"GPS means global positioning system," Elton explains.

"You mean the little screen on the dash that gives directions?" Gaga says. "Yes, I do have one. It says 'Onstar.' I believe."

You grab the phone on the wall, dial 911 and give them the information on the missing Honda Element.

"What will become of me?" Gaga whines. He runs back upstairs to the lab and looks around frantically. "I've got to take my notes and leave."

Before you can stop him, the professor is heading back down the stairs. The door at the bottom slams and you hear the lock turn.

"Wait a minute! He's just locked us in!" Elton exclaims.

"Why?" Mina asks.

Suddenly, there is a sound like a nail gun firing, once, then twice. A man howls out in pain, then silence. Then Mr. Angel's voice floats up the stairwell.

*Turn to page 32.*

"Brains," he says. "More brains."

"When did Angel come back? No one is going to believe this," Mina says.

"Do you think he just killed Gaga?" Elton asks.

"Well, Gaga's awfully quiet if he's alive," Mina snaps.

Elton finds a crowbar and starts to work on opening the door. "We have to escape."

"If we could only turn back time," Mina says putting her head in her hands.

You pick up a syringe, and fill it with purple reanimation serum. "The Professor will be right as rain," you say, holding it up.

"In no time," Mina says, smiling half-heartedly.

Suddenly the doorjamb gives. "I've got it!" Elton exclaims, holding up the crow bar in triumph. "Just like the movies."

From somewhere below you hear the same word repeated.

"Brains."

"Let's get out of here," you all say at once.

**The End**

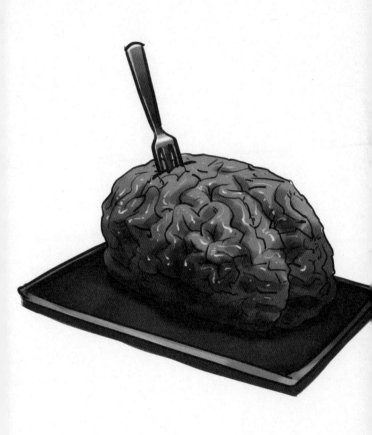

You stay on the main path but lose sight of Rose. The rain is falling hard washing out her bike tracks.

"What do you think she's doing in here?" Mina says.

"Maybe she heard the same noise we did and decided to investigate," Elton wisecracks. Up ahead you see a bike leaning against a gravestone. "That must be her bike," Mina whispers. "She can't be too far."

There is a blinding flash of lightning. Followed by a loud CRACK! The figure of Rose Laplante is suddenly silhouetted against the angry storm sky. She looks like she is praying in front of a gravestone! Then it goes dark.

"There she is!" Mina says.

"I saw her too. Let's go," you agree.

A nervous-looking Elton tags along. You all three stumble through the rough grass, past several rows of gravestones, heading in Rose's direction.

"I think she was in this row," Mina says. "In fact I'm positive."

*Turn to page 36.*

You have to agree with Mina. "She was in front of that one! The one with the cross," you cry. "But she's gone."

You hurry over to the gravestone where Rose was standing and stop dead. Mina joins you and gasps.

"Does that say what I think it says?" Elton asks weakly.

The tombstone has no dates and a single name:

# DESJARDINE

*Turn to page 40.*

"Rose—or Sam if that's who she really is—can't have gone very far," you say. You scan the hillside of tombstones. But it's too dark to see much. She could be hiding behind any one of them.

There is another flash of lightning. It's followed in less than a second by a thunderous BOOM!

"That one was less than a mile away," Mina says.

"Hey, look!" you say, pouncing on a folded up paper on the ground in front of the Desjardine tombstone. "It's a printout of a train schedule. It's the last train from Boston to Pointy Hill."

Mina and Elton look over your shoulder.

"And by my watch it gets here in less than 15 minutes," Mina says. "The paper is barely wet. Rose must have dropped it, and my bet is that she left to meet that train."

*Turn to page 70.*

You decide to decline Gaga's invitation.

"Uh, thanks Professor, but it looks like you're busy," you say.

"Yeah," Elton adds with a wave. "Looks like you're in the middle of something important."

"How dare you! You can't just LEAVE!" Gaga yells. "Not after interrupting me!" He begins to waddle down the steps. The three of you make a run for it, out the front door, across the yard and up the street. A dog barks in the distance, and a light comes on. But you just keep running. Several blocks away, when you have covered enough ground to feel safe, you stop.

"That was close," Mina says.

"That guy is a total freak," you add.

Elton, who spends more time in front of a computer than at the gym says nothing and just gulps for air.

"Where to next? Back to the cemetery for Rose?" you suggest.

"Sounds like a plan," Mina agrees.

You begin to retrace your steps, this time at a walk. Suddenly a passing car pulls over and honks.

*Go on to the next page.*

"Mom!" you cry. "What are you doing in that car?"

"Mine's in the shop. And it's more like what are you doing out on the street when you're supposed to be home for dinner? Hop in. I'll give Mina and Elton a ride home," she answers.

You glance at Mina and Elton and shrug.

"Guess the party's over for now," you say. "We'll have to look for Rose tomorrow."

Your friends nod and the three of you pile in for the ride home.

You mom looks in her rearview mirror.

"What were you three up to in this weather, anyway?" she asks.

You look at your friends and get a devilish idea.

"We were spying on our science teacher Professor Samuels. First he stole our dead shop teacher's body from the cemetery next to Elton's house. Now he's upstairs in his home lab trying to turn him into a zombie," you say nonchalantly.

Your mom is pretty cool so she plays along.

"So, just another crazy night in Pointy Hill, Maine then?" she replies, chuckling.

**The End**

"So Rose *is* Sam!" you cry. "Samosa Desjardine. My old penpal!"

"It's starting to look more likely, I've got to admit," Elton agrees.

Mina scans the horizon. "But where did she go?"

"I'll give her one thing," Elton says. "She's got guts to be in here alone in this kind of weather. And at this time of night."

Suddenly you hear the mysterious scraping sound again. Followed by another "plomp". You look at your friends.

"Could that be her?" you wonder.

Mina shakes her head. "I doubt it. We heard that noise from that direction over there, and just seconds before we saw Rose at this tombstone. She can't be in two places at once."

"Maybe it's a special zombie power? To be in two places at once?" Elton offers. "Why don't we go back to my house and look up zombie powers on the internet?"

Mina ignores Elton. "If you want to continue to look for Rose, I'm in. But I would be interested in finding out what's making the scraping sound. Your call. She's your long lost penpal."

*If you go to investigate the noise,*
*turn to page 9.*

*If you decide to continue to look for Rose,*
*turn to page 37.*

Mina looks into the darkness after the ghost of the car that has disappeared into the night. "He doesn't have a home," she says. "He's the living dead."

"You there!" Professor Gaga calls.

"Wait where you are," Mary Brown screams, her voice deep and booming.

"Just like a gym teacher," Elton says, shaking his head in disgust, "always giving orders."

"Let's get out of here," you say.

It's not hard to outrun the two adults. Everyone knows Mary Brown is the most out-of-shape gym teacher in Maine. The three of you trot in the direction of the big highway that leads out of Pointy Hill. But you don't go eight blocks before you find the Volvo. The car is crumpled against a tree, liquid is oozing from the gas tank, one headlight is on and the right turn signal is blinking. Mr. Angel sits in the driver's seat staring into the darkness. Everything is silent for a moment, then, somewhere a frog begins croaking, a mouse squeaking, blackbirds swoop across the face of the Wolf Moon.

*Turn to page 42.*

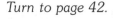

"Helllllll," Mr. Angel says, "oooooooo."

"We'll get you out, Mr. Angel," you say, rushing forward. "Hang on."

He looks at you, tries to smile, waves his stump in your direction, "Ommmmm," he says, just before the car catches on fire.

Suddenly there is a loud flash and you are in a beautiful place where everything smells like sweet flowers, like roses, everything is a rose. Apples are roses; the sky is a rose; the rose of the lake is reflected in the rose of the sky and the place where Mr. Angel sits smiling at you, happy at last, is a rose.

And you, of course, are a rose.

**The End**

"Okay, let's start by examining the facts. Our science teacher is a grave robber," Elton says.

"The question is why would anyone want the body of our shop teacher, Mr. Angel?" Mina wonders. "I mean people rob graves for valuables, or artifacts, or...."

"Experiments," Elton states.

"That's it," you say, snapping your fingers. "It all makes sense. This must be one of Professor Gaga's wacko experiments."

"What can we do?" Mina says.

"We have to call for help," Elton says.

*Turn to page 44.*

# 44

"No one will believe three kids who call in to report a grave robbing," Mina says, "The police will just think it's a prank."

"We'll just have to stop him ourselves then," you say.

Mina looks up at the moon in the sky, "You know this full moon is known as the Wolf's Moon. In my moon calendar it's also called 'The moon of tragedy,' but we're not superstitious."

Ignoring Mina, Elton says, "Do you think he might take Mr. Angel's body back to Dragonfly?"

*Go on to the next page.*

"If he's planning some experiment he has a fully equipped lab there," you reply. "No one will be around in the middle of the night."

"Sounds logical," Elton agrees.

Mina rolls her eyes. "Thank you Spock."

The shortcut to your school is through the pine woods just east of the cemetery. When you get there, a light is on in the windows of the science room.

"He's here all right," Elton says.

"You mean, they're here," Mina corrects. "Look."

A figure emerges from the shadows of the science wing. In the bright Wolf Moon you can clearly see it's Mr. Angel, looking pale, walking stiff-legged with clods of dirt dropping from his new burial garb. . .

"It looks just like him but that can't be Mr. Angel," Mina says, "I just don't believe it."

"It's Mr. Angel all right," Elton says, "Look. He's missing half of his left hand. Remember, he lost it while teaching us how to make bird feeders?"

"The table saw accident," Mina says.

*Turn to page 46.*

# 46

"He nearly died that time," you say.

"So he was dead this time but now he's alive?" Mina looks upset.

"No. Now he's the zombie woodshop teacher," Elton says. "That's different than just plain dead."

Mr. Angel has reached Professor Gaga's old Volvo station wagon. He hits his head twice on the door frame before he manages to get inside the boxy car. The engine turns over and the lights come on. Behind the wheel Mr. Angel concentrates on staring straight ahead while using his good right hand to maneuver the vehicle.

As he steers the car toward the exit, a man and a woman run into the parking lot waving their arms and yelling, "Stop! Stop, Adam, please! STOP!!!"

"Mr. Angel's first name is Adam?" Elton says.

"It looks like their experiment is out of control," you say.

"That's Mary Brown," Mina says, shocked. "Now our gym teacher is in on it?"

*Go on to the next page.*

The car has turned around. Mr. Angel is now heading toward your hiding spot in the trees. You step out from behind a tall spruce tree and wave your arms, signaling for Mr. Angel to stop. In the distance, Ms. Brown and Professor Gaga spot you and turn in your direction. Mr. Angel brakes and, because he can't roll the window down without a hand, pounds on it instead. When the side window breaks, he tries to smile but his face is a little crooked and some dirt still clings to his chin. His right eye keeps blinking like a malfunctioning shutter.

"Haaaaaaaaaaaaaa," he says.

"What do you think haaaaaaaaaaaaaa means?" Elton says.

"I think he's trying to say 'hi'" Mina says.

"Where are you going, Mr. Angel?" you ask. "Can you tell us where you're going?"

"Ommmm," he says, and then, "Bah-bah."

"Ommmm? Does he mean home? Who is he now? E.T.?" Elton asks.

Mr. Angel waves his left stump hand one more time and accelerates over the divider and onto Sunny Way. The car turns west towards the big highway that leads out of town. Driving away into the darkness, the Volvo tail lights become two fading red beacons.

"He wants to go home. Wherever that is, poor guy," Mina sniffs.

"Shouldn't we chase after him?" Elton asks.

*Turn to page 48.*

# 48

You point in the direction of Ms. Brown and Professor Gaga who are getting closer.

"We are about to have other things to worry about," you say.

"I really hate Wolf Moon nights," Mina says.

"Me too. I say we chase Angel," Elton agrees.

*If you go after Mr. Angel to stop him, turn to page 41.*

*If you decide to confront Professor Gaga and Ms. Brown, turn to page 50.*

Mary Brown shouts at the three of you as she barrels forward. "Stop right there! What are you doing here?"

As usual, she is wearing simple, practical, dark clothing over her enormous body. Her legs are round as telephone poles with breadbox-sized shoes attached.

"We're observing the Wolf Moon in action," Mina replies.

"Sure you are," Mary Brown sneers. "Ralph, where should we put them?"

"How about the cages in my lab at home?" Professor Gaga replies, panting from the run. "The question is what we do with them?"

Mary looks surprised, and snaps, "For a scientific genius, you can be a real birdbrain. We'll remove their souls, of course, and add them to my collection."

*Go on to the next page*

"You mean we'll be able to control them like the others?" Professor Gaga says.

The others?

"Now you're catching on," Mary Brown states. "I already have your little friend Rose's soul," she adds looking directly at you. "I am her master."

"But you're not my mas...."

Before you can finish your sentence, Mary Brown has sprayed you with a potion.

"I thought that was fabric softener," you whisper before passing out.

You awaken in Gaga's lab. Or at least that's where you think you are. It is dark outside. You are locked in a metal cage. Looking around you see Mina and Elton. They are still unconscious. The sound of voices drifts up the stairs.

"Where do you keep the souls?" you hear Professor Gaga ask.

"In my gym locker at school. I keep them in a red plaid thermos bottle," Mary Brown answers. "No one would think to look in a thermos."

"All of them?" Gaga queries.

*Turn to page 53.*

"Thirty-eight last count," Mary Brown replies with satisfaction. "Although these days I need to keep their names on a list to keep track. With my memory, it's all I can do to control one or two zombies at a time."

"Tomorrow we'll extract the three new souls that are up in the lab," Professor Gaga says. "I can't wait to see how it's done."

"At first light," Mary Brown says.

"Like love!" Professor Gaga says.

"No, that's 'love at first sight,'" Mary Brown sighs.

You hear a door close. Outside a car engine turns over, then starts. You see car headlights through the attic window; the sound of the engine grows faint.

"Hey! Everybody! Wake up! This is our chance," you cry. "We have to get out of here and collect some souls."

Mina and Elton roust slowly.

"What are you talking about? Where are we?" Mina asks, looking around. "My head aches."

"We're at Gaga's lab. I just heard them discussing Mary Brown's zombie collection. She keeps the zombies' souls in a plaid thermos in her gym locker," you report. "She has thirty-eight of them and I bet Rose is one."

"How are we going to get out of here?" Elton asks, rattling his cage.

"I have a skeleton key," Mina offers, pulling it off a ribbon around her neck.

*Turn to page 54.*

"For the same reason you keep a yo-yo under your bed. Emergencies," Mina replies.

You try the key on the lock to your cage. With a little work and some twisting, there is a loud click, and the door swings open. You open the other cages, releasing your friends. "Now we have to get out of here and get that thermos of souls before they do."

"I think we're too late," Mina says, peeking from the attic window. "They just pulled in."

"But they don't have the plaid thermos," Elton says, peering over Mina's shoulder. "It looks like Chinese take-out."

The three of you tiptoe down the stairs and listen at the door.

"Smells like Chinese take-out," Elton sniffs. "Makes me hungry."

"How can you think of food at a time like this?" Mina snaps.

There is the rattle of utensils as the table is set. Dishes clang. Someone puts on some Frank Sinatra, and cranks it.

"Now is our chance. Come on," you say.

You quietly open the door to the lab, cross the living room, and slip out into Gaga's yard unseen. Frank Sinatra's voice floats into the yard, smooth as butter.

*Go on to the next page.*

"Let's go get the souls," Mina says.

"Mary mentioned keeping a list. I'm sure she keeps it with the souls in her gym locker," you say. "After all she's a gym teacher."

At Dragonfly School you find Mary Brown's locker. There is a picture of a large fire-breathing dragon on its door with the school cheer GO DRAGONS painted in all caps.

Sure enough, the plaid thermos is there.

"Let's get out of here," you say, sticking the thermos under your arm, "before we're caught."

"Wait," Mina says. She pulls off an envelope taped to the locker ceiling and opens it. "Could this be her list of soul donors?"

"If it has thirty-eight names, I would say yes," you reply.

Mina quickly scans and counts. "It does! And Rose is one of them!"

---

*If you decide to find Rose—who might really be Sam—to see if she knows how to get her soul back from the thermos, turn to page 66.*

*If you decide to return to Elton's house to figure out your next move, turn to page 61.*

"Let's go check school first," you decide. "Gaga sometimes works in the lab there. And it's on the way to his house anyway, right?"

But when you get to Dragonfly, the science lab on the third floor is dark. There is no sign of Gaga's Volvo in the parking lot.

"Let's check his house," Mina says. "I know where it is. I babysit the Carter kids three doors down."

"After you," you say.

Mina takes you and Elton on a couple of short-cuts to Wayland Road. Just as you turn the corner on to Gaga's street, there's a loud BANG followed by glass exploding.

Lights come on in houses up and down Wayland Road. But the house with the dented Volvo wagon in front is curiously quiet. Plus it has smoke pouring out the top floor windows.

"Gaga's place?" you ask Mina. She nods.

"Looks like his experiment went wrong," Mina says flatly.

"People still have electricity," Elton says. "Look. Everyone is standing out in their yards. Cool."

"Wow," Mina points, "Mrs. Yakker remembered to put on her robe but forgot her teeth."

*Go on to the next page.*

In the distance you hear a siren, then the sound of horns as the big fire trucks approach.

"Come on," you say. "It's now or never."

"What? Where are you going? Are you crazy?" Mina asks, running after you as you duck into a neighbor's yard, run across the back lawn and yank open Gaga's kitchen door.

"This is the only way we'll find out what happened to Mr. Angel!" you cry. You run inside and follow the smell upstairs.

Gaga's upstairs home lab is nothing but a charred box with wet burnt paper peeling from the walls. He sits on a chair in the middle of it all. His face is blackened with soot, and his hair stands on end.

"I survived the explosion," he says. "My Bomb Proof Total Immortality Formula works! I'm alive! I have defied death, won the big chess game, defeated the grim reaper."

"But are you okay?" you ask.

"Where's Mr. Angel?" Mina asks, but Gaga ignores her question.

"I'm better than okay," the professor shouts, "I'm immortal! My formula will make death a thing of the past."

*Turn to page 58.*

"Just stay calm, professor," you say. "The fire and police people are here and an ambulance is on the way." You can hear someone out front with a megaphone.

"No need for an ambulance," Professor Gaga announces grandly. He stands up but has trouble keeping balance.

"Why don't you sit back down, Professor?" you suggest in your most calming voice.

"You don't believe me?" The Professor's voice sounds tight in his throat.

"Sure, sure I do," you say. "We all do. Mina, Elton and me."

The professor is not convinced. He picks up a small brown wooden box with a red handle on the side. "Mr. Angel made the box for me," he says. "Its pine with a cedar lining. I call it Pandora. It makes a very loud noise when you press the little handle. Look around, you can see the results."

"Just be calm," you say, "Don't do anything…. Why don't you give me the nice box?"

You reach your hand forward slowly.

## KABOOM!

Unfortunately for you and Mina and Elton, Gaga's Bomb Proof Total Immortality Formula still needs a bit of work. Too bad!

**The End**

You decide to go back to Elton's house to figure out what to do with Mary Brown's thermos of souls. After you grab some cold lasagna that Elton's mom has left out for you on the kitchen counter, you retreat to the study to discuss the situation.

Mina, who has been studying the list of names from Mary's locker, is perplexed.

"These are all kids from school," she says. "A few are in high school now. And Billy Baffert has moved away. But what's the connection between them?"

"I'll tell you the connection," Elton says between bites. "They're all pale, with a dazed look, sunken eyes, and an appetite for fresh brains."

Mina rolls her eyes. "Very funny."

You grab the paper and study it.

"I actually don't think they're zombies yet. From something Mary Brown said tonight. Wait! I think I know. Isn't everyone on this list in the Dragonfly Chorus?" you ask.

"No wonder their last concert sucked pond water," Elton says.

Mina snaps her fingers. "And the connection is that Mary Brown sometimes subs for the pianist who practices with the chorus. She would have access to these kids, but no one would suspect her of anything. Everyone associates her with athletics."

*Turn to page 62.*

**62**

"How can we get their souls back to them?" you ask, holding up the thermos. You have opened it up for a look. It's filled with pungent brown soul juice that looks a lot like maple syrup.

"Easy," Elton replies. "Spike their lemonade at practice tomorrow morning."

Mina smiles broadly and pinches Elton's cheek, making him blush. "I knew there was a reason we were friends."

That night you and Elton and Mina work out a formula to redistribute the soul syrup to the chorus. You make sure to leave enough for the four people who have gone on to high school and Billy Baffert. You'll get their souls back to them later.

Luckily, Operation Lemonade goes off without a hitch. There's just one little problem. When you get back to Elton's house, the extra soul juice is missing.

Mina calls from the kitchen, "Where did you put the thermos, Elton?"

"I stuck it in the fridge," Elton says.

"Well, I can't find it," Mina says, "Come take a look for yourself."

You and Elton go into the kitchen.

*Turn to page 65.*

The thermos is gone. "Maybe your little brother took it?" you suggest.

"Thomas?" Elton bellows up the stairs.

"What?" His voice has authority, deep without the squeak in it that was there yesterday.

"Have you seen the thermos that was here on the counter this morning?" Elton asks.

"The red plaid one?" Thomas calls down the stairs.

"Yeah," Elton replies. "Where is it?"

"I have it up here," he says. "It's empty though."

"Empty," Elton says. "What do you mean empty?"

"Empty, like there's nothing in it anymore," Thomas answers.

"What happened to the stuff that was in it?" Mina asks.

"It tasted pretty good," Thomas says, "I was dying of thirst and there wasn't any juice. Sorry."

"Does his voice sound somehow deeper?" Mina says.

"More adult," Elton agrees.

"Those soulless people won't know what they're missing," you suggest. "I hope. I mean, have you heard anyone at school complaining?"

"Maybe they can grow new ones?" Elton says hopefully.

**The End**

"I think we should get Rose's soul back to her first," you say. "Let's head to my house and try calling her."

Mina and Elton agree, so you set off. As you approach your house, you are surprised by the sight of Rose herself sitting quietly on your front porch steps. She stands up as you approach.

"I...I know you do not know me well, but I have been sent here to find you. Someone who is trying to...to help me...said I would be safe here with you," Rose says.

"One question first. Are you really Samosa Desjardine, my old penpal from New Orleans? The one who everybody called Sam?" you blurt out.

Rose knits her brow in deep worry. "I think I am. Yes. People used to call me Sam. When I was little. Until Mad Mary took me away. I just know that I need help, whoever I am."

"Mad Mary! You mean Mary Brown our gym teacher is Mad Mary from your letters?" you cry.

Just then a car turns onto your street. Rose, or Sam, suddenly looks terrified. "Who is that?" she cries.

"Come inside," you say, quickly opening your front door.

*Go on to the next page.*

The four of you hustle inside and lock the door. Luckily, your parents are out to dinner. And your mom has left two large pepperoni and mushroom pizzas with a note that says "in case you brought the gang back with you!"

"Are you hungry, Sam?" you ask.

She glances around nervously as the car passes by. "Yes, but do you have any raw meat?"

"So you really are a zombie," Elton says in wonder.

Sam nods. "Fresh brains are almost impossible to find. That's what zombies really need. But raw meat keeps me from starving."

"How about getting your soul back first?" Mina suggests.

"My soul?" Sam asks. She slumps down. "Mad Mary has it."

"Not anymore," you announce, pulling the plaid thermos out of your backpack.

Sam's eyes bulge. "Where did you get that?" She reaches her hands toward it.

"Watch out," you warn. "According to Mary Brown, there are thirty-eight souls in there."

Sam carefully unscrews the lid of the thermos and takes a sniff.

Then she hands it back.

*Turn to page 69.*

"I cannot take my own soul back," she says. "Someone else has to give it to me."

You measure out a dose for Sam. "I guess you just drink it," you say. "I'm not sure."

"That makes sense to me," Elton says.

"Me too," Mina adds.

Sam takes the small glass from your hand and drinks. She wrinkles her nose.

"What does it taste like?" Elton asks.

"Cabbage juice," Sam says. "It tastes awful."

"Drink the rest," Mina urges.

Sam takes the glass, holds her nose and drains the rest of the liquid.

"Yuk," she says with a shiver and a grimace.

"Do you feel any different?" Mina says. "Is it working?"

Sam's eyes are closed. As you watch, beginning at her feet, her skin begins to turn robin's egg blue. The color suffuses her body. Then just as quickly she becomes bright as liquid gold, before returning to her normal skin color.

"What a show," Elton says. "Way to go rainbow girl."

Sam has a big smile on her face, "You have saved my soul. I'm human again."

"Nice to meet you, Sam," you say.

"Nice to meet you too," she says smiling.

## The End

Ten minutes later the three of you enter the Pointy Hill train station. But Rose isn't inside.

"I think I saw her on the way in," Elton says. "She looked like she was hiding."

"Hiding where?" you ask.

Elton leads you back outside. He points across the street to the bandstand in the middle of the village green. "It's Rose. Or Sam. Or whoever she is," he whispers. "In the gazebo."

You can hear the train approach.

"Why isn't she inside where it's warm and dry?" Mina wonders.

The train comes to a stop. You can hear people getting off. Every time the moon appears through the clouds, you can make out the shadow of Rose/Sam waiting. She doesn't move an inch.

A few business types emerge from the station and get into their cars, heading home to supper. The train whistle blows and a conductor calls, "All aboard!" before the train rumbles on.

Finally, when everything is quiet, a strange-looking man appears.

*Turn to page 72.*

## 72

The man is tall and very thin, skeletal almost. Even in the poor light, you notice his deep set eyes. He scans the bucolic scene of downtown Pointy Hill, barely giving you and your friends a glance. Then he steps off the station porch and into the street toward the town green. He sniffs the air. The tall man lets out a strange low bark. On cue, Rose timidly makes her way out of the shadows and comes forward.

As she nears, the man begins speaking to Rose in a strange language. There are words of English mixed in with French words and other words that come from a language you have never heard before in your life. He sounds angry. He points at a paper, tapping it furiously. Then he says some words you *do* understand: "320 Meadow Way".

Mina and Elton both look at your in surprise. That's your address!

*If you step forward and ask the man what he wants at 320 Meadow Way, turn to page 74.*

*If you decide to stay quiet and see what the strange visitor and Rose do next, turn to page 115.*

"Wait!" you cry, stepping out of the shadows to approach Rose and the tall, strange man. "320 Meadow Way is my house. That's where I live."

Rose, who is already pale, goes even paler. The man sizes you up.

"So you are the penpal of Samosa Desjardine?" he demands.

"Yes. I am!" you reply. You turn to Rose. "How do you know that? Are you…?"

"Yes, I am Sam. I used to be known as Samosa. And you were my penpal," she says shyly. She looks at her feet like she does not know what to say next.

Both Mina and Elton gasp.

"Why do you call yourself Rose Laplante?" you ask. "And who are you?" you ask the man.

"Call me Mr. Samedi," he replies. "I am here on important business. You need to take my friend to your house to be safe. While I take care of the luggage and other matters."

"I don't get it," you say. "What other matters? What does Sam need to be safe from?"

"Just do as I say," the man says. He picks up his small suitcase and begins to walk away.

*Go on to the next page.*

"Where are you going?" you cry.

"I am staying at the Old Mill Inn. You can reach me there if you spy any trouble," he answers. "Now please take little Sam to 320 Meadow Way."

Why does the name Mr. Samedi ring a bell? This whole situation is totally weird.

A cab pulls up, the tall man named Samedi gets in and says, "Stay out of trouble, you hear? I'll keep in touch."

The cab pulls away, heading down Chestnut Street in the direction of the Old Mill Inn.

*If you take Sam to your house at 320 Meadow Way, turn to page 76.*

*If you decide to follow Mr. Samedi to the Old Mill Inn, turn to page 107.*

# 76

You watch Mr. Samedi drive off. You turn to Sam and your friends.

"It's getting late. I guess we should probably take a cab," you say.

"Good idea," Mina and Elton agree. "We should all be getting home. You can drop us off on the way."

You have never taken a cab in Pointy Hill in your life, but you feel this is the right thing to do. As if by magic, the headlights of an automobile sweep the train platform. A taxicab pulls up next to where you stand with Samosa, Mina and Elton.

"This is weird," you say. "You want a cab and one appears."

*Go on to the next page.*

But the cab is almost sinister-looking. It's purple with yellow lightning bolts on the doors. Green pom-pom fringe hangs from the ceiling. You even wonder if it's safe. But, you do need a cab. And they aren't exactly plentiful in Pointy Hill at night.

"Need a ride?" the driver asks, leaning out the window. You notice several strands of beads hanging from the rear view mirror, as well as a strange assortment of what look like chicken bones on a string.

This cab looks like no other you have seen. You notice that Sam seems wary too.

*If you decide this cab looks okay for a quick ride home, turn to page 79.*

*If you decide the cab looks too creepy and offer to call another one, turn to page 104.*

You say goodnight to Mina and Elton, who decide they'd rather walk, and climb into the purple cab. As soon as the door is shut, the driver pulls away.

"Don't you want my address?" you ask.

"It's 320 Meadow Road, right?" the driver replies.

"Yes," you say. That's odd. Even though most people in Pointy Hill know each other, you've never seen this driver before. Sam has a frightened look on her face.

"What is it?" you whisper.

"Nothing," she says. "Only in one of my dreams there is a taxi, and…." Her voice trails off. "It is nothing," she says.

You are surprised at how pale she looks.

The cab turns onto Sunny Way. You notice a man outside holding a nail gun. He walks stiffly, bumping into things. For a minute you could swear it's your former woodshop teacher Mr. Angel. But he died in a table saw accident a few days ago.

*It couldn't be Mr. Angel. Weird.*

"I need your help," Sam suddenly says.

"Sure," you reply. "What is it?"

*Turn to page 80.*

# 80

"I am less alive than I used to be," Sam whispers. She looks furtively at the driver, but he has started listening to music and ignores you. "My skin has grown pale. I feel cold all the time, the warmth has left my hands. I tell you I am a walking husk."

This kind of talk begins to disturb you. Maybe Sam has some medical problem that cannot be treated, or maybe she's dying.

"You sound kind of down," you say, "but I'll help, if I can."

"Yes, I am down," Sam agrees. "What I am about to tell you, I fear, is unbelievable. Please don't laugh at me."

"I won't," you say truthfully. "I promise."

"I have lost my soul," Sam says.

"What do you mean your soul?"

"The life essence in me," Sam says. "Mary Brown is an evil woman. She took my soul, my identity, for her own personal power. She is an evil *bokor*. As long as she has my soul trapped she can control me. I've got to find it and get it back. This is why I need your help."

"I must be dense or something," you say, "Mary Brown the gym teacher stole your soul? What's a *bokor?*"

*Turn to page 82.*

The taxi crosses over a cobblestone bridge onto Cemetery Lane. The road is bumpy. You hear the river Sticks rushing under the bridge. The driver has the radio turned up to a song by Outkast. It's so loud, it shakes the hula bobble doll on the dash.

You look around, out the window.

"Wait a minute! This isn't the way to Meadow Road," you say.

The driver turns off the cracked pavement onto a rest area. "Man you want to meet will be here in a few minutes," he says.

"We don't want to meet anyone, especially not here," you reply. "What's going on?"

"I'm just the driver," the cabbie says. "I was paid to haul you across the river. Didn't ask for details, don't want them now. The good news is the ride has been paid for, tip included."

"Who are you?" Sam says.

"Like I said, I'm your driver. If you need a name, call me Bobby. Bobby Charon."

Samosa leans over, whispers in your ear, "We must get away now," she says. "This is a matter very serious. Mary Brown is very powerful."

*Go on to the next page.*

You don't understand what is going on. You feel Sam is right. You have to make a choice, maybe a life or death choice.

*If you and Samosa slip from the cab into the stand of maples behind Pointy Hill Cemetery, turn to page 84.*

*If you stay in the cab to meet the stranger, turn to page 119.*

You open the back door of the cab and scurry into a stand of silver maples nearby. Bobby Charon is drumming on his steering wheel to the beat of the music and doesn't hear you.

"Okay. Tell me what's going on, Sam," you whisper as soon as you are out of earshot.

"The honest truth? It sounds crazy, but I think I'm a zombie," Sam answers.

"Come on. They're just in books and movies!" you say.

"Maybe in your culture, but in my culture, they exist. I feel I may be one. A very powerful *bokor* has messed with my soul. I feel it's been stolen," Sam says flatly.

"I don't understand this *bokor* stuff" you say.

"A *bokor* practices the dark magic. Some people call it Voodoo," Sam says. "A *bokor* uses powders made from dried plants and animals in their rituals. The concoction used on me contained the skin of a toad from Haiti."

*Go on to the next page.*

"Someone sprinkled you with it and stole your soul meanwhile?" you ask.

"It is more complex than that. My flesh was opened, and the skin scraped, so that the powders would work. Candles were burned and songs sung. The *bokor* said it would cure me of my fear of dying. It did much more than that," Sam says.

"Wait. Was this what you wrote about it in your last penpal letter? Your Mammaw taking you to a *bokor* just before Katrina?" you cry. Suddenly all the pieces slip into place.

Before Sam can answer, you hear voices coming from the direction of the cab. Bobby Charon is talking to a woman. You cannot make out the words, but she sounds angry. And the voice sounds familiar. Staying low, you creep forward. The moon is full, bright, and casts a pool of light over the cab. Charon is holding up his hands and shrugging his shoulders. The woman's back is turned so you cannot see her face. But her shape you would recognize anywhere.

"It's Mad Mary! Our gym teacher. What is she doing here?" you whisper to Sam.

*Turn to page 86.*

"She is the *bokor*," Sam says. Her eyes fill with tears.

"Our gym teacher is a Voodoo priestess?" you ask.

"Not only that, when Mammaw disappeared during the floods, Mary took me away. She tells people she adopted me, but it's a lie," Sam adds.

A gust of wind shakes the trees, and a cloud slips over the moon as Bobby Charon gets back in his cab.

"Is that what Mr. Samedi is here for? To help you?" you ask.

Sam nods fervently. "There is going to be a showdown. His magic is very strong. Stronger than Mad Mary's. I hope."

*You hope? Geez.*

Mary Brown turns and faces the stand of maple trees where you hide. She peers into the woods and you crouch even lower. After staring in your direction for several seconds, Mary Brown utters a strange incantation. It sounds like the language used by Sam and Mr. Samedi at the station. You don't understand a word of it. Then Mad Mary gets into the cab, and drives away. You watch as Bobby Charon ferries her back across the river.

"We need to get you to my house so you're safe," you say, turning to your friend.

*Go on to the next page.*

But Sam has fallen into some kind of trance.

"Bonokonobonokonono," she chants. Suddenly she leaps up and begins to run after the cab.

"Sam! Stop!" you cry, scrambling after her.

You hope Bobby Charon doesn't look in his rearview mirror.

*If you decide you have to run after Sam and follow the cab that contains Mad Mary, turn to page 88.*

*If you decide that you have to do whatever it takes to stop Sam from following the bokor and get her some help, turn to page 95.*

You jump up and follow Sam, who is running frantically after the cab with Mad Mary. But neither of you can run as fast as a car. When you reach the other side of the bridge, the taxi is gone. Sam stares into the dark night, tears rolling down her cheeks.

"Are you sure you want to go after Mad Mary?" you ask.

Sam shakes her head. "I do not want to go after her. But that is the problem with being a zombie. I have no choice. The *bokor* controls me. She placed a spell back there. I have to follow her."

"Do you know where she went? Can you feel that too?" you ask. You peer into the night.

Sam pauses, but shakes her head. "I cannot tell. But we must start looking," she says.

"Well, Bobby Charon has a cab, and there's only one cab company in Pointy Hill," you say. "Let's start there."

You walk back to town and locate The Run Down Town Taxi Experience Taxi Company. The dispatcher is asleep at his desk.

A loud cough does not wake him so you give him a shake. "Mr. Hogg, wake up."

*Turn to page 90.*

Mr. Hogg snorts awake in the middle of his snore intake, "Wha...the money is in my sock drawer, dear..."

"Wake up, Mr. Hogg," you repeat.

Jumping to his feet, Mr. Hogg, as if blind, calls out, "Who is it, who's there?"

"It's me Mr. Hogg," you say, "and my friend Sam."

"What do you want?" Mr. Hogg says, "It's late, do you need a taxi?"

"No, we're looking for one of your drivers," you say. "His name is Bobby Charon."

"No driver by that name," Mr. Hogg announces. He holds a clipboard in his hand. "Do you have the cab number?"

"No," you say.

"Then I can't help. You could check out back if you'd like," he answers.

As you leave the building you spot a dark taxi parked near the fence. "That's it," Sam says. "Look at the bumper sticker."

Aside from the wild paint job, you notice that Bobby's cab has a sticker that says, "Zombies are people too". But someone has crossed out the word 'are' and written 'were'. Now the sticker reads, 'Zombies ~~are~~ were people too."

*Turn to page 92.*

You peek inside but the cab is empty. Then a small sound, a mouse squeak, startles you. A mouse is standing on its hind legs in the driver's seat.

"Oh my!" Sam says, "Mary was very mad. She's turned Bobby Charon into a mouse."

"That couldn't be Bobby," you say. But the way the mouse looks at you, and shakes its tiny little paw in your direction, makes you wonder if you're wrong. "How did she do it?"

Sam picks up the mouse and shrugs, "Another *bokor* power. Shapeshifting. Poor Bobby, we'll take care of you."

"Hey, you kids get away from that cab." Mr. Hogg is watching you from the office window.

Sam hands you the mouse.

"Ow!" you cry. "Bobby Charon the mouse just bit me!"

Sam's eyes are wide. "Are you sure? That's not good."

As soon as Sam says this, you feel a strange tingling all over. "Why?" you ask. "What can happen?"

*Turn to page 94.*

You hear a crow caw overhead. Strange, you think, to hear a crow so late at night. The Beatles song Blackbird begins firing through your head.

You turn to ask Sam if she knows the song. But Sam is gone. There is a big black dog standing in her place.

Someone picks you up and puts you in a tight dark space. You are quite uncomfortable and have trouble breathing. Where are you, anyway? Where's Sam?

Finally you come to a stop. Someone scoops you out and puts you on the ground. Were you in someone's pocket? You breathe deeply. The smell of mint is strong. The night air is dense with sounds. You look around. Soon the milkweed pods will burst, sending out beautiful white threads. And the leaves are already turning orange, red, and yellow. Life here on the riverbank could not be more beautiful.

Insects are abundant, even as winter grows close. At night you fall asleep to the sound of the river turning the rocks in their bed. Standing on a lily pad you puff out your chest, look up at the moon and croak out a song. "Froggy went a courting and he did ride, took miss mousy by his side...."

"Could you please just shut up," Bobby Charon, the mouse, says. "Just shut up."

**The End**

You run after Sam, finally catching up to her on the far side of the bridge. The taxi has disappeared from sight. Large tears roll down Sam's cheeks.

"Sam," you say, "I am not entirely sure what's going on. But one thing I do know is that you have to stay away from Mad Mary. Mr. Samedi told me to keep you safe. So we're going to Mina's house. She lives right nearby. We'll figure everything out when we get there."

Sam nods but follows you reluctantly

You take a shortcut through the cemetery to Mina's house. But when you get there all the lights are out.

"What are we going to do?" Sam asks.

"Follow me," you reply. "I know a secret way in though the screened porch."

You follow a ribbon of moonlight to the back. On the porch you find the secret panel, release the slide, push it down, and the door swings open. "Like magic," you say. Inside a small portion of the room is disguised to be a bookcase, but when you push a hidden latch, it swings open into Mina's room.

*Turn to page 96.*

# 96

"What's going on?" Mina, wearing her pajamas, shines a flashlight at you.

"We need to hide out for a while," you whisper. "It's serious. Mad Mary the gym teacher has stolen Sam's soul."

"She pretends to be a gym teacher but she's really a *bokor*, a Voodoo priestess," Sam adds tearfully.

"So you really are a zombie? Wow," Mina says.

You quickly tell Mina the highlights of Sam's story.

"That's terrible," Mina says.

"Yes. It's no fun being one of the undead," Sam agrees as she flops into a chair.

"Can you turn us into zombies?" There is a slight edge of fear in Mina's voice.

"I think I can," Sam says. "If I bite you, the zombie poison in my system might change you. I'm not sure."

"But you wouldn't bite us, right?" Mina says.

"Oh no," Sam says, "no, no, no, unless...."

"Unless?" Mina says.

*Turn to page 98.*

"Mad Mary made me," Sam says. "When I sleep she has control. She can order me to do anything. Which is why I must get my soul back."

"Where does she keep it?" Mina asks. "Your soul I mean."

"With lots of others," Sam replies. "In a plaid thermos that she hides."

"But once you find it how do you put it back?" you ask.

"That's why Wonder Samedi is here," Sam answers. "He will know what to do."

There is a faint rustling sound outside, like the wings of birds taking flight. Mina gestures to be quiet.

There are people whispering outside.

Sam's eyes grow round, and her hands shake uncontrollably. "I'm afraid it's *bokor* Brown."

"Someone else is with her," Mina says.

"The little man," Sam says, "He was with her in New Orleans. The little man, with the big glasses. She called him Professor Gaga."

"Gaga!" Mina exclaims.

Sam's shaking becomes violent. Her eyes are roll up into her head, her legs stiffen, she moves in a slow trance around the room.

"Bokononobokononobokono," Sam chants.

*Go on to the next page.*

"It sounds like she's speaking in tongues," Mina says. "We need to get her to a hospital."

"Wait," you say. There is another sound outside, the sound of a car coming to a stop. A light flashes on the window curtains. Someone gets out and next you hear some scuffling.

*If you try to get Sam to a doctor by sneaking out the secret passage, turn to page 100.*

*If you decide to go outside and see what is happening, turn to page 122.*

"We have to get Sam help," you say.

"Right," Mina agrees. "You go out the secret way. I'll stay here and try to distract whoever's outside."

"Be careful," you warn your friend.

You grab a coat to throw over Sam, hoping to calm her down. When you turn around Sam has changed. She's heading for you, her arms outstretched, her lips drawn back from her teeth. Her eyes look empty, like two white globes.

"I think we're in trouble," you say, just before Sam reaches you.

"Ouch," you cry, "you bit me."

Sam slumps to the floor, releasing her teeth from your left arm.

"That really hurt," you say, checking the wound.

Mina looks at you and then your bite. "Are you okay?"

"I feel okay," you say.

"Brains," Sam murmurs.

Just then, there is a loud knock on the front door.

"You both need a doctor now," Mina says. "Use the back. I'll get the front door before they wake my parents." She grabs her robe, and leaves.

*Turn to page 102.*

# 102

You haul Sam up into your arms, open the sliding panel, and slip out into the night. Sam feels very heavy. A squeaking sound comes from Sam's pocket.

*What on earth is that?*

You walk up Mina's street, in the direction of the Pointy Hill hospital. This has been quite the adventure: meeting your old penpal, finding out she's a zombie, and then being bitten. At the end of the street you decide to take a short cut through Hackett's orchards so you can reach the Emergency Room sooner. You notice that Sam is much lighter. In fact, she weighs no more than a book. Checking your arm again, you notice that the bite has healed.

*That's impossible; she only bit me ten minutes ago.*

All the excitement has made you a little hungry. *Funny, all I crave is a plate of brains.* You decide to stop so the two of you can take a little rest. You look at Sam; she is awake now, smiling at you.

"I could use a bite to eat," you announce.

"Yes. You're one of us now you know," she says, "one of the living dead."

"I'm still hungry," you reply.

*Go on to the next page.*

"For brains?" Sam asks.

"Yes. I've never had them before but all of a sudden they sound delicious," you answer. "Let's head over to Elton's house. He lives very near."

Sam's laughter frightens the birds. They flush into the night sky, outlined by the enormous moon.

"We'll never be the same again," you say.

"Isn't it lovely to think so," Sam replies.

**The End**

# 104

"Thanks," you tell the strange cab. "My mom will be here any minute to pick us up. We don't need a ride."

"Whatever," he says with a shrug.

The cabbie drives off slowly, giving you a strange look in the rearview.

"Why did you say your mom was coming?" Mina asks.

"That cab didn't feel right," you say. "That guy gave me the creeps. Look, there's another."

The next cab looks fine. It's driven by the mother of a friend. You and Sam drop Mina and Elton off before heading back to your house for the night. When you get there, your parents are out.

"Don't worry. You can sleep in the guest room," you say. "I'll just leave my parents a note." You try to hide a yawn. It's late, and your eyelids feel like sandpaper, you're so tired.

"We're going to sleep?" Sam says. She looks scared.

"Yeah," you say. "Don't worry about Mary Brown, she's just a gym teacher. She may be mean but I don't believe she is about to hurt anyone."

"Does she know where you live?" Sam says.

"It's a small town," you say, "she knows where I live, but she doesn't know we're together."

*Go on to the next page.*

"I hope you are right," Sam says.

"Trust me," you say.

Once Sam is tucked into bed in the guest room you know you have to make a decision. You can't stop thinking about all that's happened. You still have questions about the man named Mr. Samedi. You wonder if he is dangerous to your protector...

*If you stay home and make a phone call, turn to page 106.*

*If you leave the house and go to check on Mr. Samedi by yourself, turn to page 107.*

# 106

When you're certain that Sam is asleep in the guestroom, you make sure the house is locked up tight. You check the windows and doors, and pull the shades down. Outside the wind has picked up. Up the road, in the graveyard, a blackbird calls out.

You go over to your father's desk and pick up his phone, dial the number that you have dialed so many times. You cannot help yourself now, you don't want to but it is beyond your power. You hear the other phone begin to ring, then a click, slow breathing, then someone says, "Yes?" in a deep voice.

"Mary," you say.

"Call me Ms. Brown."

"Ms. Brown," you say, "she's asleep."

**The End**

You get Mina to take care of Sam, promising to call later, and follow Mr. Samedi to investigate.

Ten minutes and a cab ride later, you stand facing the Old Mill Inn. There are lights in the sitting room downstairs. Most of the upstairs rooms are dark. In one bedroom on the first floor, near the back of the house, a light shines.

You climb the steps to the front door and peek into the public rooms. Although a small fire glows in the grate, no one is enjoying the flickering coals.

Rumor is that the inn is haunted. From time to time, a guest sees a man out walking a pig on a leash. Another rumor says there's hidden treasure in the Old Mill Inn. They say that when it was an operating mill, the owner—a real penny pincher—hid a fortune in gold coins somewhere in the building.

Now, here you are outside the inn sneaking around, wondering who is this strange man Mr. Samedi? And wondering if Sam really is a zombie.

You see something move in the bushes behind the inn. It might just be the wind. The path to the back of the house is lined with ceramic gnomes. At least you think they're gnomes, although they do look a lot like dwarfs.

*Turn to page 108.*

# 108

"What do you think? Gnomes or dwarfs?" someone asks in a low whisper.

"Sam! You frightened me!" you cry as she emerges from the bushes. "What are you doing here?"

"I was afraid to be alone," Sam says, "Have you figured out which is Mr. Samedi's room?"

"Well, you scared me; don't do that again," you warn.

"That's what zombies do," she says. "We frighten people. Is it the room in the back with the light?"

"I think so," you say. "Follow me."

The two of you move like shadows. The windows in the old Inn are high off the ground. "We'll need something to stand on," you say.

Sam leaves for a moment returning with a plastic milk crate. She may be a zombie, but she's clever.

Peeking into the room you see the skeletal figure of Mr. Samedi. He slicks his gleaming black hair back with a brush, then picks up a black cloak and wraps it around his shoulders. The cloak is hooded, and you watch as he pulls the hood up, obscuring his face.

"What's he doing?" Sam says.

*Go on to the next page.*

"It looks like he's dressing up for Halloween and he's going as the grim reaper," you reply.

When you turn back to the window, the room is empty. You climb down from the crate. "He's gone," you say.

"Where do you think he's going?" Sam asks.

"I don't know," you say. "We could follow him."

"Or wait until he leaves and check out his room," Sam says.

Sam seems different suddenly, less scared.

*If you decide to toss his room, to see what you can find, turn to page 110.*

*If you decide to try to follow Mr. Samedi, turn to page 117.*

# 110

You and Sam decide to investigate Mr. Samedi's room. The night has turned ominous and the storm has returned. Clouds cover the moon and stars. In the distance thunder rumbles, spears of lightning link earth to sky in sudden shafts of energy. Electricity crackles in the air.

You sneak into the inn. Somewhere a happy sleeper snores. The house cat rubs against your leg before arching his back in a midnight stretch.

"How will we find his room?" Sam says.

"It's in the back corner, I think," you say. "I never knew this old place was so big."

You listen at several doors leading off the hallway near the back of the house.

"This one is quiet," you say. "I think it's his."

You try the doorknob. It turns in your hand. Opening the door you slip into the room.

"We have to be careful not to disturb anything," you say. "We don't want him knowing we've been snooping."

Sam opens the closet door.

"Look at this," she seems surprised.

"What?"

*Turn to page 112.*

"Let's go to Mr. Angel's house," Elton urges. "I want to see the look on Mrs. Angel's face when she sees Mr. Angel back from the dead."

"Very funny, Elton," Mina says.

You head in that direction. But when you get to the house with a sign on the lawn that says "Angel Residence" and a sign next to the doorbell that says "Where No Angel Fears to Tread", there's no sign of the Volvo. You ring the doorbell anyway.

A nice looking woman in a pink pantsuit comes to the door.

"Can I help you?" she asks.

"Ur..uh..we.." you begin.

"We were just looking for…" Mina says.

"We were wondering if you happened to see your dead husband wandering around recently? We think one of the teachers from school has brought him back to life," Elton suddenly blurts.

Mrs. Angel smiles pleasantly.

"No, I haven't seen him recently," she replies, pulling out a shotgun. "You're the second group of wiseacres who have been by this week. The next ones get shot. Make sure to tell your friends. Now scram!"

## The End

The closet is filled with large dresses in a floral prints. "Pretty weird," you agree. "Maybe they're used in some kind of Voodoo ceremony."

"What about these?" Sam holds up a glass of water with a set of false teeth in it.

"Could we be dealing with vampires too?" You both laugh.

"I think maybe we're in the wrong room," Sam says.

"Ooops," you say, stifling a chuckle. Just then the door snaps open, and a large woman in a bathrobe, hair in rollers, fills the doorway.

"HELP!," she screams. "Someone help me! There are thieves in my room!"

"Wait, we're not thieves," you say.

"Yeah!" Sam agrees, "We're not thieves."

"They have my teeth," the woman yells. "Help me."

You look at Sam, "Maybe you should put the glass down?"

She places the glass back on the side table by the bed. "I thought you said this was Mr. Samedi's room," Sam says.

"I must have made a mistake," you say, "I think we had better make a run for it, before the police arrive."

*Turn to page 114.*

# 114

You try to scoot out the window but don't make it. The manager has you in his grasp. He locks you in his office. You overhear him say, "Yeah, just kids, probably looking for the lost treasure. Yeah, yeah, gave Mrs. Klump quite a scare they did. We'll hang on to them until you get here."

He's called the police! But when the detectives get to the Old Mill Inn, they don't believe a word you say. You and Sam wait in the Pointy Hill jail for your parents to post bail and take you home. Your dad does not look too happy when he gets there.

As soon as you are in the car, he turns to you and says, "This better be good. I want you both to start at the very beginning."

## The End

You, Mina and Elton exchange an alarmed glance.

"Who is he?" Mina asks. "And how does he know your address?"

"Beats me," you say. "Let's see what he does."

The tall stranger argues in his strange language with Rose for another minute. He hails a cab, and reluctantly Rose climbs in after him. The cab takes off in the direction of your part of town, but soon it's out of sight.

It takes you twenty minutes to get home. There is no sign of Rose. The next day you decide to call her house, but there is no answer. When you get back to school after the fall long weekend on Tuesday, the teacher announces that Rose Laplante has withdrawn from Dragonfly School for personal reasons.

You never see her again. But you think of her often, and wonder what would have happened if you had made a different choice that night at the train station...

**The End**

You and Sam decide to follow Wonder Samedi into the night. You creep back around to the front of Old Mill Inn just in time to see Mr. Samedi round the corner up the street. You run after him, staying a safe fifty yards behind in the shadows. He marches with purpose, as if he knows Pointy Hill inside out. He crosses through the center of town, walks up Sunny Way and turns onto Cemetery Lane.

"He's speeding up," you say.

Sam runs along side you to keep up.

There is a bend in the road as Cemetery Lane runs toward the river. When you round the bend, Mr. Samedi is gone. Right where you would expect him to be is a grey wolf. The wolf runs quickly and suddenly darts into the forest on the other side of the river.

"Where did he go?" you ask, stopping, looking in all directions. There is not another person in sight.

"Into the woods," Sam says. She points to the disappearing wolf. "To meet his match."

"That's Mr. Samedi?" you ask. "He changed into a wolf?"

*Turn to page 118.*

Sam nods. Somehow you have trouble believing what you have just seen. But since there is nothing more you can do, and it's getting late, you take Sam home with you "to keep safe" as Mr. Samedi first requested.

Wonder Samedi never returns from the forest. Eventually the meager possessions in his room at Old Mill Inn are given away to Good Will, everything that is except a plastic bag filled with strange herbs and powders. That goes into the trash.

You are not sure it's linked, but the following Monday at school an announcement is made that Mary Brown has gone missing. Several months later, her disappearance is still unsolved. Since that first night, Sam has stayed on at your house in the guest room. She has gradually become part of the family. Your parents have even made noises about "adoption".

While Sam's behavior was odd at first, gradually she has relaxed. She looks less pale and spaced out. She even eats cooked meat now instead of the raw meat she insisted on at first. As Elton says, she no longer looks and acts like a zombie.

Which is a good thing.

**The End**

"No one can hurt us here in the cab," you tell Sam. "Let's just lock the doors."

You are doing just that when a large figure lumbers across the field. It's your gym teacher Mary Brown.

"Look! It's Ms. Brown!" you say to Sam. "Everything is going to be fine."

"No it's not," Sam says. She gets on to the floor of the cab, and covers her head with her sweater. "She's evil. She's the *bokor*."

"The *bokor?*" you cry. But it's too late. Mary Brown leans in the cab window. She gives you a big smile, and throws some yellow powder in your face. It's the last thing you remember.

*Turn to page 120.*

# 120

You awake in the morning in your own bed. You look around. Was all that stuff about your penpal Sam a dream? You don't remember how you got home last night. You call Elton, then Mina, to get their take on last night's events.

"I don't know what you're talking about," Elton says.

"Probably too many cookies before you went to bed," Mina says. She has no recollection of the search for Rose Laplante. Much less a girl called Samosa Desjardine.

Down at the breakfast table, you notice the Pointy Hill weekly news sitting on the counter. The top headline reads:

## Gym Teacher's Sudden Departure Leaves Dragonfly School in the Lurch.

You pick up the paper and scan down the article. A paragraph jumps out at you:

"Just before the school break, Mary Brown announced that she and her family were moving immediately back to Louisiana and that she will therefore not be returning to her position as physical education instructor. She felt that her daughter, Rose—an extremely shy child—was being taunted by Dragonfly students. She reported that numerous students were spreading rumors that Rose was a zombie, of all things. Brown states she was surprised by the kids' meanness, as well as by 'their lack of knowledge about other cultures'."

*Go on to the next page.*

You put down the paper. While Rose looked a little like your penpal Sam, she is probably a completely different person.

The old gym teacher Ms. Brown is right. Sometimes kids can be pretty stupid and pretty mean.

**The End**

The sounds of scuffling outside get louder.

"We better go take a look, Mina, before they wake up the neighborhood," you say. "Sam, stay here, okay? We'll be right back."

Sam continues her strange chant as you slip out the door. Mina's parents have woken up from the sounds and are tying their bathrobes on as they descend the stairs. The four of you rush outside in time to see an astonishing sight. The strange tall man from the train station, Sam's friend Mr. Samedi, is body wrestling your gym teacher Mary Brown and shouting, "You let that poor girl's soul go or it's the doghouse for you!"

You notice your science teacher, Ralph Samuels, aka Professor Gaga, jumping up and down saying "Please stop! Please stop at once."

Mina's dad turns to you and says, "Mina, are these folks friends of yours?"

*Go on to the next page.*

Before Mina can answer her dad's question, a police siren approaches. Mad Mary and Mr. Samedi stop wrestling long enough for some neighbors to jump on them and split them up. The police arrest everyone and cart them down to the station. Or the "hoosegow" as Mina's dad calls it.

The next morning the police have the answers to everything except the astounding transformation of Mary Brown into a black Labrador retriever inside her jail cell in front of their very eyes.

It seems the Wonder Samedi is a powerful *bokor* indeed.

**The End**

## ABOUT THE ARTISTS

**Illustrator: Wes Louie** was born and raised in Los Angeles, where he grew up drawing. He attended Pasadena City College, where he made a lot of great friends and contacts, and then the Art Center. Wes majored in illustration, but also took classes in industrial design and entertainment. He has been working in the entertainment industry since 1998 in a variety of fields.

**Cover Illustrator: Keith Newton** began his art career in the theater as a set painter. Having talent and a strong desire to paint portraits, he moved to New York and studied fine art at the Art Students League. Keith has won numerous awards in art such as The Grumbacher Gold Medallion and Salmagundi Award for Pastel. He soon began illustrating and was hired by Disney Feature Animation where he worked on such films as *Pocahontas* and *Mulan* as a background artist. Keith also designed color models for sculptures at Disney Animal Kingdom and has animated commercials for Euro Disney. Today, Keith Newton freelances from his home and teaches entertainment illustration at The College for Creative Studies in Detroit. He is married and has two daughters.

## ABOUT THE AUTHOR

**Ken McMurtry** was born in Oklahoma. He attended colleges in California, Iowa, and Vermont. He has written several young adult adventure novels and two non-fiction books. Ken loves reading, telling stories, traveling, and spending time with his family. In the past he and his family have lived in Ireland, Spain, Italy, and Greece. When not imagining exciting adventures, Ken likes to cook, watch sporting events, exercise, and take power naps. He now lives in Vermont with his wife Polly and their two lovely goat girls Phoebe and Persephone.

**For games, activities and other fun stuff, or to write to Ken, visit us online at CYOA.com**